Astronaut Girl

MISSION TO MARS

For Christina Koch and Jessica Meir, who completed the first all-female spacewalk in Oct. 2019. Thanks for inspiring Val, us, and the rest of the world!—CH & EV

For Dave, Heather, and Matt, my bubble family—GR

PENGUIN WORKSHOP
An Imprint of Penguin Random House LLC, New York

Manufactured in China.

Visit us online at www.penguinrandomhouse.com.

Library of Congress Cataloging-in-Publication Data is available.

ISBN 9780593095805 (paperback) 10 9 8 7 6 5 4 3 2 1
ISBN 9780593095812 (library binding) 10 9 8 7 6 5 4 3 2 1

by Cathy Hapka and
Ellen Vandenberg
illustrated by Gillian Reid

Penguin Workshop

1 - un
2 - deux
3 - trois
NASA

Chapter 1

A BIG SURPRISE

"Put away your spelling books, kids," Ms. Ortiz said. "It's time for science."

"Yay!" I cheered.

My friend Ling laughed. "Okay, Val, everyone knows you love science."

"True," I said. "But today's lesson is going to be *extra* special."

Wallace and Abby looked over. "What do you mean, Val?" Abby asked.

"Yeah, what's so special about ecosystem

worksheets?" Wallace said with a grin.

Before I could answer, the classroom door opened. I stood and waved. "Hi, Mom!" I called.

I was proud of myself for keeping such a big secret. My mom was our guest speaker! She's a botanist, a scientist who studies plants.

"Pay attention, class," Ms. Ortiz said. She introduced my mom and explained that she would be teaching us about terrariums.

"That's right," Mom said. "And after that, you'll get to make your own at home!"

Everyone seemed excited, even the kids who aren't very interested in science.

Wallace raised his hand. "What's a terrarium?"

"I'm glad you asked," my mom said. "It's like a miniature garden. Here's one I made."

She went into the hall and returned with a large glass bowl with ferns and other plants growing inside.

"Cool!" a kid said. "It looks like my fishbowl, but it's full of plants!"

"That's a good way to put it," Mom said. "Fishbowls and fish tanks—also known as aquariums—are self-contained ecosystems. So are terrariums."

Wallace raised his hand again. "So is the Neutrodome," he said with a big smile. "That's the domed city Commander Neutron built on Planet X."

I rolled my eyes. Commander Neutron is a character on *Comet Jumpers*. Wallace is obsessed with that TV show. He and I even wrote a script for it and entered it in a contest.

"That's right," Mom said. "In a terrarium, you're creating your own little world."

She went on to teach us all about terrariums. The most important thing is to use plants that grow in the same type of environment. Each terrarium needs several layers. First comes a layer of pebbles for drainage. Then you add charcoal to filter the water. Next comes soil for plants to grow in. Finally you add the plants—plus any decorations you want.

When Mom finished, Ms. Ortiz stepped forward. "I hope you were paying attention, because your project is to make a terrarium this weekend," she said. "You can work in groups of three or four. Materials are in the supply closet, or you can get creative and use recycled materials from home."

I was excited to get started. Mom had lots of cool plants in her greenhouse, and I had an extra-large fish tank I wasn't using for any experiments right now.

I also knew exactly who I wanted in my group. "Let's work together," I told Wallace, Ling, and Abby.

We gathered at my desk. "I have a great idea!" Ling exclaimed.

"So do I," Abby said.

"Me too," Wallace added.

They all started talking at once. Wallace pulled out Zixtar, his homemade action figure. He wanted to turn our terrarium into a science fiction landscape. Abby wanted to create a colorful fairy garden. Ling just kept talking about a long-necked bottle she thought would be perfect to hold the terrarium.

"It'll be a fun challenge!" she exclaimed. "We can use tongs to arrange all the stuff inside."

"Hold on!" I shouted. "We need a plan. Let's meet in my lab tomorrow and figure it out."

My friends agreed. And I was sure I could convince them to agree to my other ideas, too!

Chapter 2

PLANS AND PROBLEMS

The next day, Daddy helped me get the big fish tank down from the shelves in the garage. “Wow, this is heavy even when it’s empty,” he said. “It’ll be even heavier once your terrarium is full of soil and plants.”

"But it's perfect for the project I have in mind," I told him. "My goal is to create a terrarium using only recycled materials. All the plants will be edible and also improve indoor air quality!"

Daddy carried the fish tank into the kitchen. "That sounds great, Val, but shouldn't you ask the rest of the team for input? Remember one of my favorite sayings: Many brains working together make the best science!"

Daddy *does* say that a lot. He works with other supersmart scientists. He's an astrophysicist—a scientist who studies outer space—just like me. That's why my nickname is Astronaut Girl.

I thought about what Daddy said as we carried the tank into my basement lab. But before I could answer him, we heard the doorbell and hurried back upstairs. Wallace was at the door.

"Look what I brought!" Wallace said.

He was carrying a box. Inside were several Venus flytraps in pots that were usually on his bedroom windowsill.

They're carnivorous plants, which means they eat bugs. Last week, Wallace showed me how to feed them dead flies.

Zixtar was in the box, too—along with a

mini Zixtar made of clay. There was also something I didn't recognize.

"What's this?" I asked, picking it up.

Wallace grinned proudly. "I made it for our terrarium," he said. "It's a planetary rover with laser beams and a giant claw to fight off aliens."

Daddy chuckled. "Sounds like you're ready to create another episode of *Comet Jumpers*."

"I'm always ready for that!" Wallace exclaimed. "Hey, Val, that reminds me—we should hear back about the contest soon!"

The show wanted people to send in ideas for future episodes. But Wallace and I—with a little help from his friend Carlos—had written a whole script instead. I was excited about the contest, too. But right now I was more focused on our science project.

"We can't use those," I told Wallace. "Venus flytraps need totally different growing conditions than herbs."

"Herbs?" Wallace said while making a face. "This is supposed to be a terrarium, not an herb garden!"

Mom came into the kitchen holding my baby brother. "Can someone watch the Baby?" she said. "He's already spilled two watering cans, and I really want to finish planting the lettuce before it rains."

"Sure, he can help us brainstorm our extraterrestrial terrarium," Wallace said, taking the Baby. "He's always ready for an outer space adventure!"

He laughed loudly. My parents gave him a funny look.

"Thanks, Wallace," Mom said. She and Daddy hurried off.

Then Ling and Abby arrived. Ling was carrying a bluish-green glass bottle with a superlong, skinny neck. Sticking out of the bottle were a pair of superlong, skinny tongs.

Abby had a bulging cloth bag. "I brought some pretty rainbow-colored sand and other stuff we can use," she said.

I frowned. None of this would work with my plans! I was sure my friends would realize that once we got started.

"Let's go downstairs," I said.

I led the way to my science lab. My cat, Astro Cat, was already napping inside the fish tank. On the worktable nearby was everything we needed to create my herb garden. There was a bucket of gravel, some activated charcoal, a bag of potting soil, and several plants from Mom's greenhouse.

My tablet was sitting on top of my favorite book, *The Universe*. I picked up the tablet and opened my plans for the terrarium. "I figured out where each plant should go for optimum success—" I began.

"That's nice. I did some planning, too!" Ling exclaimed. She set her bottle next to the fish tank. "It will be really fun to put our garden inside this bottle. See? I printed out some examples from the internet."

She passed us each a handout with our

name at the top. It showed several photos of bottle terrariums.

Wallace bounced the Baby on his hip and squinted at his handout. "I didn't make mini Zixtar small enough to fit in there," he said. "But Val's fish tank would give us plenty of room to make a whole planet! I brought some meat-eating plants that look like aliens. And Val's mom has some cool spiky succulents. They definitely look like they're from out of this world!"

I shook my head. "Succulents are desert plants. They won't thrive in the same ecosystem as Venus flytraps!"

Abby looked at Wallace's plants. "These are beautiful," she said. "But they won't work in a fairy garden."

I clenched my fists. "This is supposed to be a science project!" I cried so loudly that

Astro Cat woke up and the Baby chortled. "It's not about alien landscapes or fairy gardens or cool skinny bottles!"

"But Ms. Ortiz said we can get creative," Abby protested.

Ling shrugged. "Let's take a vote to decide what to do. Who votes for my bottle garden?"

"We don't need a vote!" I yelled. "I wish this was a space mission, since I'd be the commander and you'd all have to do what I say!"

"I wish your mom had real alien plants in her greenhouse!" Wallace said at the same time, staring at his Venus flytraps.

WHOOOSH!

The Baby squealed as the room began to spin . . .

VAL
THE UNIVERSE
THE UNIVERSE

Chapter 3

WHERE ARE WE?

"What's happening?" Ling cried.

"Val, we're not in your basement anymore . . . ," Abby said.

"Don't worry, Wallace and I have done this before," I told my friends distractedly. "We seem to have landed in some sort of biodome."

"Awesome! It's like the Neutrodome on *Comet Jumpers*!" Wallace set down the Baby and pulled out Zixtar.

"I wonder where we are!" he continued.

I was wondering the same thing. Daddy always says to assess the data, so I carefully observed our surroundings. My friends, the Baby, Astro Cat, and I were in a huge, clear, round bubble—a biodome. Outside, everything was barren and reddish-brown. In the far distance, I spotted a rocky ridge much taller than anything on Earth.

"I have a theory," I said.

"Wait, what?" Ling said. "Val, what's going on?"

I quickly explained about the adventures Wallace and I had been having. "So far we've been to the moon on the Apollo 11 mission, and traveled into the future to the stars and an asteroid," I said. "I think we're in the future again, because we're in a biodome. And my working theory is that we might be on Mars—the Red Planet!"

"So cool!" Wallace exclaimed. He was making Zixtar dance around so Astro Cat could chase him. "This *does* look like a red planet."

The Universe was lying at my feet. I grabbed it to look up more information about Mars to confirm my theory.

Before I found the right chapter, Abby tilted her head. "Did you hear that?" she said. "It sounded like a dog barking."

Astro Cat heard it, too. He stood up straight, and his tail got extra fluffy. He hid behind Ling and growled.

A second later, a robot dog trotted into view. He barked twice, then spoke. "Greetings, visitors from Earth." His voice was deep, like the main actor on *Comet Jumpers*. "Welcome to the Mars Biodome. I am a Mars Universal Tech and Transport unit. You may call me MUTT."

Part of his face was a computer screen. When he spoke, the word *MUTT* flashed across it in green letters.

"Hi, MUTT," Wallace said with a salute. "A robot dog . . . cool! I hope you don't *byte*." He grinned at the rest of us. "Get it? Get it?"

I laughed. "Dogs bite, and computers byte," I said. "Good one, Wallace."

Ling rolled her eyes, and Abby looked confused.

"I'm Wallace," Wallace told MUTT, "and this is Zixtar."

The rest of us introduced ourselves, too. Then the Baby crawled forward with a giggle. "Piggy!" he cried, reaching for MUTT's curly wire tail.

MUTT spun around to avoid the Baby's grasp. "Caution, Human Infant," he said. "My tail is a very sensitive power and data interface that plugs into every system in the biodome."

The Baby giggled again. "Piggy!" he shouted happily.

Meanwhile, Astro Cat peered out from behind Ling's legs, looking suspicious. MUTT stepped closer. "Is that a feline?" he asked as Astro Cat hissed at him. "We don't have any of those here."

"Do you have other animals?" Abby

asked. “Real ones, I mean?”

“Affirmative. This biodome system is an experimental habitat for various Earth species,” MUTT replied. “The farm dome is that way.”

He pointed with his nose toward one of several arched doorways leading out into smaller domes. But I was still looking around the main dome. It looked like a huge house with no walls. There were beds, a kitchen table, lots of chairs and sofas, shelves and cabinets full of supplies, and all sorts of other stuff. Everything looked sleek and modern—especially the towering bank of computers, screens, keyboards, and other instruments in the middle.

“See, I told you guys we were in the future,” I said.

“This place is amazing,” Abby said.

"Hey, look, art supplies!" She hurried over for a better look at one of the shelves.

Ling stared outside. "I can't believe we're really on Mars," she said. "Hey, what's that? It looks like a tornado!"

We all rushed over. On the horizon, a column of churning red dust stretched as high as we could see. MUTT plugged his curly wire tail into a nearby outlet. Numbers and symbols flashed across his robot face.

"The storm is currently moving away from the biodome," he said. "There is no need to activate the protective walls."

Wallace tapped the clear, thick wall of the biodome. "Protective walls?" he said. "Isn't that what these are?"

"Negative," MUTT replied. "I am referring to additional protection to avoid sand blowing into the vents during storms."

Abby wandered toward one of the arched doorways. "Check it out, this room looks like a rain forest!"

"Really?" Ling ran toward another door. "This one's boring—it looks like the utility room at school where the fuse box and hot water heater are."

Wallace was making Zixtar dance on one of the computer keyboards. "Look, Zixtar is a scientist!" he exclaimed.

"Stop that!" I cried. "You could accidentally shut off the oxygen or something. Everyone come back here and let's make a plan to investigate the biodome together."

"Piggy!" The Baby started chasing MUTT again.

Wallace scooped him up. "Come on, Baby, let's see if there are any real pigs in this place."

"Stop!" I yelled again. But nobody was listening. My friends each disappeared through a different archway, leaving me behind.

Chapter 4

HOME SWEET BIODOME

I couldn't believe how my friends were acting. After all, I was Astronaut Girl! So why weren't they paying any attention to me now that we were actually on another planet?

"At least *you* stayed with me, Astro Cat," I said.

Astro Cat was glaring at MUTT. When I gave him a pat, he leaped straight up in the air and then fled with a yowl.

I sighed. It was just me and MUTT now.

"So, MUTT," I said. "Tell me about this place. How does the biodome work?"

"The biodome is a fully isolated ecosystem," MUTT began.

"Sort of like a terrarium," I said, thinking of our school project.

"In many ways, yes," MUTT said. "But on Mars, the outside atmosphere cannot sustain human life. The dome is carefully calibrated to provide all necessities, such as breathable air, water, and temperature control."

He trotted over to the bank of computers and plugged in his tail. A screen started flashing information about the systems that kept the biodome running. It was super interesting!

"Wow, so every system works together to recycle everything inside the dome?" I said. "It must have taken a long time to build this."

"Affirmative," MUTT said. "A team of Earth scientists worked together for many years to design and build the Mars Biodome."

That reminded me of Daddy's saying that many brains working together made the best science. It also reminded me of my terrarium team. I wished they were here to see what MUTT had just showed me.

"I should check on the others," I said. "I

wonder where they went."

"Two life forms detected in the rain forest pod," MUTT replied.

"Thanks, MUTT," I said. "Being connected is handy!"

MUTT unplugged, then led me toward the rain forest pod. At the end of a short, clear tunnel was a door. MUTT pushed it open, and humid air rushed out as we entered.

The rain forest pod was smaller than the main pod. But it was still bigger than the gym at school. It was full of plants and trees. Water poured over rocks from a high waterfall that splashed into a clear pool.

Abby was there surrounded by art supplies. She was painting Astro Cat, who was lounging beside the pool with one paw trailing in the water.

"Hold that pose, Astro Cat," Abby said.

I looked around. "Fascinating," I said. "This must be where they recycle water for the whole biodome."

Abby looked up. "Oh, hi, Val. Isn't this beautiful?"

"Sure," I said. "But listen, MUTT was just showing me how this pod works with all the others to keep the biodome safe for human life."

Astro Cat rolled over and his round, furry belly flopped into view. Abby laughed. "Wait, I need to paint this!"

I sighed. Abby wasn't listening. "Come on, MUTT," I said. "Let's check on the others."

MUTT led me to another side pod. It was full of plants, too, but they were all vegetables and other food crops. It was very bright because of several large grow lights. All the plants were growing in containers of different shapes and sizes. I spotted corn growing in an enormous square tub. Nearby were rows and rows of tall plastic tubes the size and shape of telephone poles, but with holes for plants to poke out. They stretched all the way to the top of the dome. Strawberries grew in some of them, and others held lettuce and other plants. Ling was tasting a tomato.

"Look, Val," she said when she saw me. "This is amazing! All these vegetables are growing in water instead of dirt! It's like that little herb garden your mom has in the kitchen!"

I nodded. "That herb garden is hydroponic."

MUTT barked in agreement. "The biodome food garden is fully hydroponic," he told us. "That means we grow our crops in a water-based system with nutrients added. Growing hydroponically is a much more efficient use of space and water, both of which are in short supply on Mars."

"That's so cool," I said.

But Ling wasn't paying attention. Her eyes widened. "Ooh! Are those hot peppers? I could use these to make my world-famous superhot salsa!"

"Hey, Ling, do you want to come learn more about—"

Before I could finish, Ling rushed over to the corn patch. "I love roasted sweet corn!" she cried.

I sighed. "Come on, MUTT. Let's see where Wallace went."

Wallace was in the next pod over. "This is the zoological pod," MUTT said as we entered.

I could barely hear him. The zoo pod was noisy! That was partly because it was full of all kinds of creatures—bleating goats and sheep, buzzing bees, chirping crickets, and more. It was also partly because the Baby was there chasing some squawking chickens and giggling loudly. When he saw us come in, he stopped.

"Piggy!" he yelled.

Wallace stood nearby wearing a white lab coat over his clothes. He was peering into a glass-walled habitat.

"What's in there?" I asked, walking over.

"Some really cool bugs!" Wallace exclaimed. "They look like alien monsters from *Comet Jumpers*!"

"Those are Hercules beetles," MUTT said. "They are one of the largest insects on Earth. Scientists have studied the behavior of smaller insects in low gravity since the beginning of the space program. Here in the Mars Biodome, we are studying the effects of life on another planet on many types of insects and spiders."

I looked around. A case nearby contained an ant colony. Others held spiders, fruit flies, and various creepy-crawlies.

I didn't even bother trying to convince

Wallace to leave. "Okay, MUTT," I said. "What's in the rest of the pods?"

MUTT led me past the utility pod to one that was smaller than the others. Parked in the middle was a vehicle with rugged tires and a big, domed see-through top.

"Wow, is that what I think it is?" I exclaimed.

"It is a vehicle known as HELPER," MUTT said. "That stands for Human Essential Life-sustaining Planetary Exploration Rover. It is used to explore the Martian surface."

"So it *is* a rover!" I grinned. "My friends are definitely going to want to see *this*!"

Chapter 5

HELPER

"Attention! Attention!" I said. MUTT had just shown me how to make an announcement to the entire dome system from the main computer. "Urgent meeting in the main room—come right now!"

Seconds later, Wallace skidded to a stop in front of me, holding the Baby.

"Are we being invaded?" Wallace cried. "Where are the aliens?"

Before I could answer, Ling and Abby

rushed in. Ling was holding a cucumber. A colorful square of fabric flapped from Abby's hand. Astro Cat sauntered in last.

"What's the big emergency?" Ling exclaimed.

"Is everyone okay?" Abby glanced around with concern.

"Everything's fine," I said with a smile. "Actually, better than fine!"

Ling pointed her cucumber at the fabric

Abby was holding.

"What's that?"

Abby held it up. A reddish-brown circle was painted on the fabric. It looked like a flag. "Do you like it?" she asked. "I got inspired looking at the colors outside."

"Ahem!" I said. "As I was saying, I want to show you something amazing. Follow me."

MUTT and I led the others into the transportation pod.

"Ta-da!" I pointed toward the rover. "This is HELPER. We can use it to explore Mars!"

Everyone started talking at once. Wallace looked especially excited.

"I can't believe Zixtar and I are actually going to explore another planet!" he exclaimed.

Abby waved her flag. "I'd love to get a closer look at the colors out there."

"Wow!" Ling said. "I could be one of the first kids to step foot on the Martian surface!"

I smiled. Finally, we were all excited about the same thing! "Let's start off toward that big mountain on the horizon," I said. "I think it might be Olympus Mons, which is three times taller than Mount Everest!"

"What are we waiting for?" Wallace cried. "Let's get out there!"

MUTT showed us our space suits. "There is no suit to fit you, Feline," he said to Astro Cat.

Astro Cat hissed at him and backed away. Then he ran out of the pod.

"Astro Cat can stay here and guard the biodome while we're gone," Ling joked.

"He'll be fine by himself."

"He will not be alone," MUTT said. "I will be here monitoring the weather outside in case it becomes necessary to raise the protective walls due to a sandstorm."

We put on our suits. I zipped up the Baby and looked around. "Everyone ready?"

My friends climbed into HELPER. But when I tried to follow with the Baby, he shrieked in protest.

"Piggy!" he cried, pointing at MUTT. "PIGGY! *PIGGY!!!*"

"Piggy isn't coming," I told him.

The Baby's face turned bright red, and he wiggled so hard I almost dropped him. "Stop that!" I cried over his shrieks of "Piggy!"

Ling peered out. "It looks like the Baby wants MUTT to come."

"PIGGY!" the Baby howled.

My friends got back out. "Maybe we should just bring MUTT along," Abby said.

"But he has to watch for sandstorms," I protested.

Wallace glanced outside. "No storms in sight," he said. "We won't be that long."

"But I think it would be better if—" I began.

"Let's take a vote!" Ling said. "All in favor of MUTT coming along, say *aye*!"

Ling, Abby, and Wallace said, "Aye." The Baby said, "Piggy!"

I still didn't think this was a good idea, but I was outvoted. Maybe it would be okay.

MUTT's face blinked with a series of green question marks. "This is somewhat irregular," he said. "But I was created to assist humans and I will do as you wish."

He climbed into HELPER. The Baby giggled and snuggled in next to him.

"Okay," I said, grabbing *The Universe*. "Let's go!"

Chapter 6

MARS UP CLOSE

"Now what?" Wallace said when we were all strapped into HELPER.

MUTT barked. "I will activate the airlock remotely," he said. A large door slid open, revealing the airlock beyond. "The HELPER unit is voice controlled."

"Cool!" Ling said. "HELPER, drive us into the airlock."

"Wait," I said. "We can't all give HELPER commands. That's too confusing."

Ling shrugged. “Okay, should I be in charge?”

“No!” I exclaimed. “I’m Astronaut Girl,

remember? *I* should be the commander."

By then we were in the airlock with the inside door closed behind us. The outer door started sliding slowly open.

"Let's not fight," Abby said. She waved her flag at us. "Oops!" The flag caught on something that clattered off HELPER's inside wall.

"What's this?" Wallace picked up a long metal pole with a wedge on the end.

"It looks like a digging tool," I said. "HELPER, drive us outside now."

Ling was still looking at the tool as HELPER rolled through the outer door. "I have an idea," she said. "That looks like it could be a flagpole. We can plant Abby's flag outside the biodome!"

Wallace held up Zixtar. "We think that's a great idea!"

"I don't," I said. "Sandstorms on Mars can be pretty strong. Your flag might blow away."

"No problem," Ling said confidently. "We'll plant the pole nice and deep. Come on, Abby. We got this!"

"Watch out for that low gravity," Wallace said with a grin. "You'll definitely be able to do a backflip out there!"

"Maybe, maybe not." I paged through *The Universe* to double-check my facts. "Gravity on the moon is seventeen percent of Earth's. But gravity on Mars is thirty-eight percent, so you won't be able to jump quite as high here."

I told HELPER to stop. Ling and Abby tied the flag to the pole, then climbed out onto the Martian surface outside the dome.

Wallace, MUTT, the Baby, and I watched them bounce around giggling for a few minutes. “This is fun!” Abby said through the radios in our helmets.

The two of them planted the flag. They both saluted it and did a little dance, then returned to HELPER.

“HELPER, take us toward Olympus Mons,” I ordered. I looked at my friends. “I think that’s the big mountain over there.”

“Mountain?” Wallace peered out the front of the vehicle. “It looks more like a mountain range.”

"It's all one mountain," I said, flipping through *The Universe* again. "Olympus Mons is the tallest mountain in the solar system, way taller than any on Earth. It's about as wide as the entire state of Arizona!"

HELPER moved steadily across the plains outside the dome. Plumes of reddish dust rose behind us.

Wallace looked around. "This rover is great," he said. "You can see everything!"

Ling pointed up. "Is that a moon? It's tiny!"

"Mars has two moons," I said. "Right, MUTT?"

"Affirmative," MUTT said. "The one above is Phobos. It is only 13.8 miles in diameter. Deimos is even smaller—just 7.8 miles. They are among the smallest moons in the solar system."

There was a lot to see on Mars. We looked out at vast plains, with lots of rocks and ridges. My friends were surprised that not all the rocks were red. MUTT and I explained that it's the reddish dust in the atmosphere that makes the whole planet look the same color. My friends all agreed that driving across Mars was like the coolest safari ever!

But after an hour, we still weren't that close to Olympus Mons. We decided to get out to stretch our legs.

Wallace stared up at the mountain, bouncing the Baby on his hip. Even at this distance, we couldn't see the top or either end.

"Wow," Wallace said. "It's enormous!"

I nodded. "Even though Mars is about

half the size of Earth, lots of stuff here is much bigger," I said. "The mountains are higher, the canyons are deeper." I laughed. "Even the years are bigger!"

"What do you mean?" Abby asked.

"It takes Mars 687 Earth days to travel around the sun," I said. "That means a year here is almost twice as long as one on Earth."

"So we're all younger on Mars?" Ling asked.

"Affirmative," MUTT spoke up. "If you are nine years old on Earth, you are approximately four and a half on Mars."

Abby laughed. "I'm the same age as my little sister!"

Suddenly MUTT howled loudly. HELPER's lights all flashed and an earsplitting siren sounded.

"What's going on?" Wallace cried as the Baby looked surprised.

"Return to HELPER immediately!" MUTT ordered. "A severe sandstorm has been detected. We must return to the biodome!"

Chapter 7

OUTRUNNING THE STORM

We scrambled back into HELPER. The Baby squealed with excitement as Wallace strapped him in.

"Back to the dome, HELPER!" I cried. "Top speed!"

Abby peered out the back as HELPER's engine roared to life. "I don't see anything coming yet," she said, her voice shaking.

A map appeared on MUTT's face screen. It showed our location with a dot. The dust

storm was marked by a tornado-shaped icon. “It is coming this direction,” MUTT said. “There’s still a thirty-one percent chance that we can reach the biodome before the storm reaches us.”

“Thirty-one percent?” Ling exclaimed. “I don’t like those odds!”

By then HELPER was moving so fast that the scenery was a blur.

"Whee!" Wallace cried, clutching Zixtar. "This is fun!"

I checked the instruments. "We're going at least four times as fast as before," I said. "We should reach the biodome in fifteen minutes. That might be fast enough to outrun the storm."

Then I looked at MUTT's face screen

again. The storm icon was moving faster than the dot.

"Or maybe not," I said with a gulp.

The others looked at the map, too. Nobody said anything, but everyone looked nervous.

I glanced out the back. Nothing yet. But I knew the storm was coming.

HELPER sped over the reddish plain, dodging boulders and bouncing over sand dunes. Would we make it? I counted down the time—still ten minutes out. Then nine, eight, seven, six . . .

Suddenly MUTT barked. "Storm incoming!"

As I leaned forward to check the map, Wallace spun to look out the back. "I see it!" he shouted.

We all turned to look. The horizon had

been swallowed up in a stormy sea of swirling red dust. It swooped forward, and seconds later, we were surrounded by a churning cloud of sand particles, dust, and small rocks. We couldn't see much through the windows, but we heard *pings* and *thumps* as debris struck HELPER's thick glass and metal sides.

Abby covered her head with her hands. "This is like the hailstorm that hit us when my family was camping," she moaned. "I thought the tent was going to be ripped to shreds!"

"That will not happen to HELPER," MUTT reported. "Its exterior is built to withstand harsh Martian conditions. But it would be preferable to reach the biodome as soon as possible."

He could say that again! I peered forward. The clouds of dust parted briefly.

"I see it!" I cried. "I see the biodome!"

"Awesome, we made it!" Ling exclaimed.

"Well, not yet," I said. "It's still off on the horizon."

Wallace flinched as something big *thump*ed off the windows. "What was that?" he cried.

"I don't know," Abby said. "But I hope we get back soon."

I hoped so, too. A Martian dust storm was no joke!

I held my breath. We were only three

minutes out. Then two . . .

"What's that?" Wallace shouted.

I turned to look out the back and saw a towering column of spinning dust, miles high, interlaced with crackling pops of electricity, like hundreds of tiny lightning bolts.

Abby's eyes went wide with terror. "It's coming right at us!" she cried.

"That is a sand tower," MUTT said. "It is similar to an Earth tornado, though much, much larger. The moving dust and sand can become electrically charged. That's one reason for the protective walls back at the biodome."

I caught another glimpse of the biodome. It was only about fifty yards away.

"We're almost there!" I cried. "How close do we have to be to open the airlock?"

Before MUTT could respond, the sand tower engulfed us. Now it was impossible to see anything but swirling sand and crackling electricity. We huddled together.

"Almost there," I whispered.

Suddenly a bigger flash arced toward HELPER and hit the front with a sizzle. Abby screamed, and the Baby gurgled in surprise. HELPER's instruments all went dead, and the vehicle stopped short.

Chapter 8

A SCARY DECISION

"What happened?" Ling cried.

"An electrical jolt shorted out HELPER's power system," MUTT said. "HELPER is no longer operational."

Abby looked outside anxiously. The sand tower had passed, but the storm was still raging. "Does that mean HELPER might fall apart?"

"Negative," MUTT replied. "The exterior remains strong enough to withstand any

potential hazard on Mars."

"The same thing happened on episode one hundred and fourteen of *Comet Jumpers*," Wallace said with a nervous laugh. He held up Zixtar. "Commander Neutron got trapped in a plasma storm on Planet Polliwog and survived by sheltering in his hoverpod. Maybe we should wait here until the storm passes."

"Good idea," Abby said.

I shook my head. "*Not* a good idea. We need to get inside and put up the protective walls before the storm destroys the entire biodome!"

Ling gasped. "Val's right! We'll have to run for it!"

"Are you kidding?" Abby said. "We're safe in here! And the dome is still so far away!"

Wallace peered out through the swirling storm. "It's not *that* far. Probably not even the length of a soccer field."

Ling put her arm around Abby. "We can do this," she told her. "We'll stick together, and it'll be fine."

I was worried—Abby still looked really scared. I wasn't sure we'd be able to convince her. "Ling and I could run over by ourselves," I suggested.

To my surprise, Abby shook her head. "No, you guys are right," she said, her voice shaking. "We should help one another through the storm."

"Great, let's go." Wallace stuck Zixtar in his space suit pocket. "I'll carry the Baby."

We unstrapped ourselves. "Can you open the airlock from here?" I asked MUTT.

"Negative. We are too far out," MUTT replied. "But I will initiate the opening sequence when we are close enough. The outer door will stay open for one full minute before closing to allow the inner door to open. That means you will have limited time to get inside, so it is imperative that you do not stop for any reason."

Ling laughed. "Yeah, guys," she said. "Don't stop to take any selfies with the dust storm!"

We all smiled, even Abby. "Everyone ready?" I asked. "Make sure to stick together. We can do this!"

I reached for the emergency release on HELPER's door. As soon as it swung open, red dust and small stones rushed in and whipped around inside the vehicle. I jumped out and waved my arm to tell the others to follow me.

Fighting my way through the dust storm wasn't easy. Strong wind gusts tried to knock me over, like one of those TV weather reporters during a hurricane. It was hard to see through the gritty reddish dust blowing against my helmet's

VAL

faceplate. Debris spattered my space suit, filling every nook and cranny of the fabric.

Every step took a huge effort. But I kept putting one boot in front of the other. Closer, closer . . .

Finally we were just a few yards from the airlock. The two huge doors were sliding slowly open.

"Almost there!" I yelled.

I glanced back. Wallace was right behind me with the Baby. Abby was close, too. MUTT and Ling were bringing up the rear.

The doors were all the way open now. That meant we had one minute to get inside. We were going to make it!

I put on a burst of speed and dove into the airlock. The wind was still swirling around in there, but it wasn't as strong.

Wallace jumped in with the Baby. They

were both smiling. Wallace high-fived me.

"Come on, Abby," I yelled. "You're almost home free!"

A sudden gust almost knocked Abby over, but she caught herself and rushed in. I grabbed her hand to help pull her to safety.

Then we looked out at the others. MUTT was almost to the door, and Ling was only ten feet behind him. The doors were already sliding shut, but they both had plenty of time to get inside.

MUTT trotted in. "Piggy!" the Baby cheered.

I looked back at Ling—just in time to see something fly out of nowhere and wrap itself around her helmet! She staggered and stopped, trying to push the item away.

Abby gasped. "That's my flag!" she

cried. "You were right, Val. It blew away!"

"You're almost here, Ling!" Wallace shouted. "Follow my voice!"

"She can't," I exclaimed. "Your voice is in her helmet! And now she can't see which way to run!"

Ling was spinning in circles, still trying to claw away the flag blocking her view.

I glanced at the doors. They would snap shut in less than fifteen seconds. "Hang on, Ling!" I cried, leaping for the opening. "I'm coming!"

"Negative," MUTT said, blocking my

path. "I shall rescue the human."

He galloped back out into the storm. Wallace, Abby, and I watched anxiously as he reached Ling and gave her a shove toward the closing airlock doors.

"That way, Human," MUTT ordered.

Ling stopped spinning and charged forward. Wallace reached out and grabbed her hand, yanking her the rest of the way in.

Whew! She was finally safe!

"Hurry, MUTT!" I yelled. "Get back in here!"

MUTT sped toward the door. It was almost shut. Would he make it?

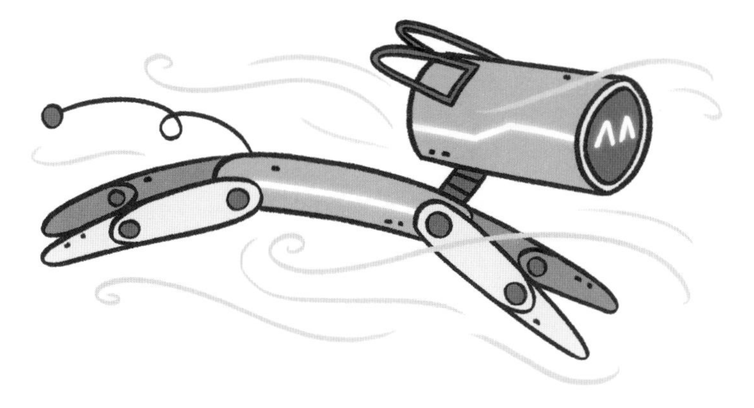

He did! He leaped forward just as the doors closed behind him with a loud *snap*.

"Yay!" Wallace cheered.

"Piggy!" the Baby cried.

But I was staring at MUTT's rear end. The doors had caught his curly tail—and snapped it right off!

Chapter 9

SAVING THE BIODOME

"MUTT! Your tail!" I cried. "It's gone!"

"Affirmative," MUTT said.

The Baby crawled closer. "Piggy," he said sadly.

Now the others saw it, too. "Yikers!" Wallace said. "Maybe Abby and I can sculpt you a new tail out of clay. Do you want a dog tail or a horse tail?" He laughed. "Or how about a peacock?"

"This is no time for jokes," I snapped. "That wasn't just a tail. It was how MUTT connected to the entire biodome system!"

Ling's eyes widened. "Then how can we put up the protective walls?"

"Exactly," I said grimly. "MUTT, do you have any ideas?"

"Affirmative," MUTT said. "One of you will have to input the command manually. I will show you which keyboard to use."

We shed our space suits and hurried into the main dome. Astro Cat was there, curled up on one of the bookshelves, with a pile of books scattered on the floor beneath him. When we came in, he woke up and hissed at MUTT.

I rushed to the bank of computers. MUTT told me which one to use and

helped me figure out the coding. Working together, we found the command to raise the protective walls.

"It's working!" Abby cried, pointing outside. "They're going up!"

The protective walls were huge! They emerged out of the reddish ground and slid up smoothly, despite the blowing dust and grit still raging around them. Soon they surrounded the entire biodome, shielding it from the storm.

"Whew!" Wallace said as lights blinked

on all over the biodome to make up for the lack of daylight. "That was close."

"Yay, the biodome is safe!" Ling cheered.

MUTT's face flashed. "Biodome status unknown," he said. "It is necessary to do a manual check to see whether any damage was done to the automated systems."

"Good point," I said. "How do we check that?"

"Normally I could plug into the mainframe to get the information," MUTT said.

"Great!" I said. "That means I should be able to code my way in."

When I tried, I couldn't get into System Control even with MUTT's help. "The system must be damaged," MUTT said. "Even with my tail intact, it would take a long time to fix."

“But if we can’t check with System Control, how do we know if anything else is damaged?” Abby asked.

“What if the air system is broken?” Wallace exclaimed at the same time. He staggered over and collapsed onto the sofa. “I think I might feel a little faint!”

“Not possible,” I told him with a sigh. “Even if the system was broken, the oxygen wouldn’t be running out yet.”

Wallace sat up and grinned sheepishly. "I feel better already!"

I turned to MUTT. "Can we check the systems manually in the utility pod?" I asked.

"Affirmative. I will show you how."

We rushed to the utility pod and looked over all the instruments and dials. The good news? The air and temperature systems were okay. The bad news was that a few of the secondary systems, like the ones controlling food and water in the smaller pods, were no longer functioning.

"Oh no," I exclaimed. "If things aren't fixed quickly, the plants and animals will die! A biodome only works if all the parts work together. MUTT, we need to hack into that mainframe somehow!" I dashed toward the main computer, then stopped short when I noticed MUTT's missing tail. "Or maybe I should try to build you a new interface tail. I could probably figure it out if I look at the blueprints on the system. No, that might take too long." I spun around to stare at the computer. Then I glanced toward the farm pod and gulped. "Nothing can survive without water for very long . . ." I took a deep breath. "I have to focus. I'm Astronaut Girl, and Astronaut Girl always figures out what to do!"

"Val, stop!" Ling cried, grabbing my arm. "You're Astronaut Girl, but you're not in this by yourself."

"We want to help," Abby added.

Wallace nodded. "We'll figure out what to do."

I realized my friends were right. I didn't have to do this all by myself.

"Daddy says many brains working together make the best science," I said. "That means they're a team, and so are we. I guess I forgot that." I smiled at them. "I know we can fix this—together."

We quickly came up with a plan: We'd tackle the problem in two teams. Abby and I worked together to fix MUTT's tail. I handled the technical aspects with MUTT's help. Abby was an artist, and whenever she made sculptures, she first made an armature—a wire frame that acted like a skeleton for the clay. She had fun creating a new tail out of the wires I gave her. The Baby stayed with us, keeping a close eye on his piggy friend.

Meanwhile, Wallace, Ling, and Astro Cat worked to keep the plants and animals happy. Wallace tossed hay to the goats and sheep and carefully dropped food into each tank of creepy-crawlies. Astro Cat helped by chasing the chickens away from the other animals' food until it was their turn to be fed. Ling adjusted the water and

fertilizer levels in the hydroponic farm pod, and sprinkled fish food in the pond while checking the humidity in the rain forest pod.

Would our teamwork save the day?

Chapter 10

TEAMWORK

We all crossed our fingers and toes as MUTT plugged his shiny new tail into the main computer. His face lit up with flashing numbers and letters.

"It works!" I cried.

My friends cheered. Wallace made Zixtar dance. Even Astro Cat didn't hiss at MUTT for once.

"Piggy!" the Baby cried gleefully.

"Can you fix everything now?" I asked MUTT.

"Affirmative," MUTT replied. "It will take a bit of extra time, but I can do it." His face flashed more numbers. About ten seconds later, he barked. "Systems fully operational."

Wallace laughed. "That really was a *bit* of extra time," he said. "Get it? Like bits and bytes?"

I ignored him. "Let's make sure everything came through okay."

We split up to check the pods. I took the utility pod, where everything looked good. When we met up again, my friends reported that the other pods were fine, too.

"We didn't lose a single fruit fly," Wallace said proudly.

"We did it, guys!" Ling exclaimed.

Soon after that, MUTT announced that the dust storm had passed and it was safe to lower the protective walls. Before long we could see the vast red landscape of Mars again.

"Gorgeous," Abby said.

"It's been fun being the first kids on Mars," Ling said. "Too bad we can't take a picture to show everyone."

"Photography is one of my functions," MUTT reported.

"Cool!" Wallace exclaimed. "Mars selfie!"

We all posed in front of the window. When MUTT took our picture, the flash

1st KiDS ON Mars!

was so bright that I closed my eyes. When I opened them, we were back in my basement lab!

"Whoa!" Ling said. "What happened? I blinked, and suddenly we're back here!"

Abby looked disappointed. "We didn't even have time to get MUTT's photo to help us remember Mars."

I gasped. "I just had a fantastic idea for our terrarium!"

Before I could tell them my idea, we heard footsteps on the basement stairs. It was Daddy.

"Hi, kids," he said. "Val, you and Wallace just got a package from California."

We rushed upstairs. The package was from the *Comet Jumpers* producers! We ripped it open. Inside were T-shirts, tote bags, hats, stickers, and even a couple of

mugs with the show's logo on them.

"Wow, this is amazing!" Wallace exclaimed. He stuck Zixtar in one of the mugs and zoomed it around, pretending it was a spaceship. "Does this mean we won the contest?"

I was already scanning the letter that was in the package. "Not exactly," I said. "They're not going to use our script. But listen to this!"

Ling, Abby, Daddy, and the Baby gathered around. Astro Cat was sitting in the box, ignoring us all. "What is it, Val?" Ling asked.

I took a deep breath. Wallace was going

to love this! "*Comet Jumpers* is going to name three new characters after me, Wallace, and Zixtar!"

Wallace's jaw dropped. He almost dropped Zixtar, too. "This is the greatest thing that has ever happened to me!" he said. "Happy dance!"

We all joined in the happy dance with Wallace and Zixtar. Even Astro Cat!

"Who's next?" Ms. Ortiz said that Monday at school. "Val, would your group like to present your terrarium?"

"We'd love to!" I stood and looked at my team. "Let's go."

We fetched our terrarium from under Wallace's desk. It looked amazing—we'd created an alien landscape out of fully recycled materials.

"It's meant to represent a scientifically possible alien planet," I explained.
"See? These are Earth plants known as succulents, but they look strange, like alien plants might. We got them from my mom's greenhouse."

Wallace spoke next. "I made this planetary rover out of clay. Val helped me model it after the real rovers that NASA has sent to explore Mars." He grinned and winked at the rest of us, and I knew he was thinking about our adventure.

"I created the sand and stone layers," Abby said. "The top layer is red sand, but there are lots of other colors layered underneath."

Ling went last. "I was in charge of finding just the right container," she said. "I chose this dome-shaped bottle, which reminds me of a biodome I saw once." Now it was her turn to wink at the rest of us. "Fitting stuff through the top of the bottle also made it more challenging and fun."

When we finished, the whole class clapped. Ms. Ortiz smiled. “Wonderful job, kids,” she told us.

I grinned at my friends. “Thanks,” I said. “We do make a pretty great team!”